To Jill, whose family claimed their ancestors were
Viennese . . . but really, Blinshers —D.P.

To Jessica, who I love even more than garlic . . .
which is a lot —A.R.

This book was drawn in ink with a forsythia reed pen, along with a steel nib.
The colors were painted with gouache.

Cataloging-in-Publication Data has been applied for and
may be obtained from the Library of Congress.

ISBN 978-1-4197-4681-9

Text copyright © 2020 Daniel Pinkwater
Illustrations copyright © 2020 Aaron Renier
Book design by Pamela Notarantonio

Published in 2020 by Abrams Books for Young Readers, an imprint of ABRAMS.

Printed and bound in China
10 9 8 7 6 5 4 3 2 1

Abrams Books for Young Readers are available at
special discounts when purchased in quantity for premiums
and promotions as well as fundraising or educational use.
Special editions can also be created to specification.
For details, contact specialsales@abramsbooks.com
or the address below.

ABRAMS The Art of Books
195 Broadway, New York, NY 10007
abramsbooks.com

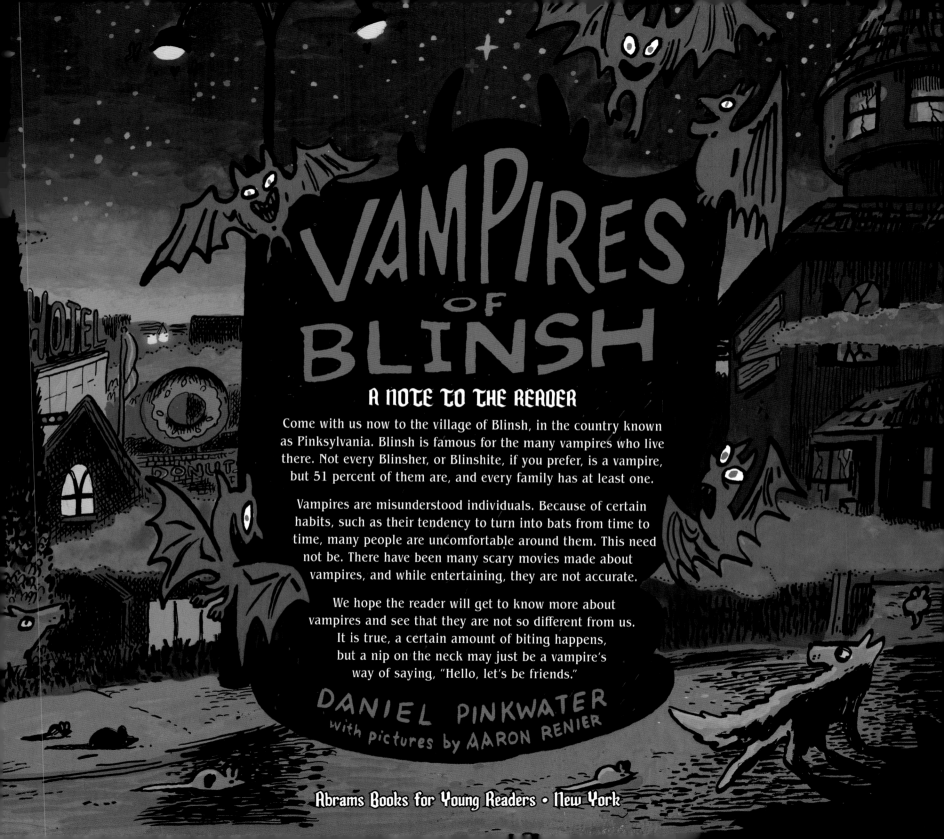

VAMPIRES OF BLINSH

A NOTE TO THE READER

Come with us now to the village of Blinsh, in the country known
as Pinksylvania. Blinsh is famous for the many vampires who live
there. Not every Blinsher, or Blinshite, if you prefer, is a vampire,
but 51 percent of them are, and every family has at least one.

Vampires are misunderstood individuals. Because of certain
habits, such as their tendency to turn into bats from time to
time, many people are uncomfortable around them. This need
not be. There have been many scary movies made about
vampires, and while entertaining, they are not accurate.

We hope the reader will get to know more about
vampires and see that they are not so different from us.
It is true, a certain amount of biting happens,
but a nip on the neck may just be a vampire's
way of saying, "Hello, let's be friends."

DANIEL PINKWATER
with pictures by AARON RENIER

Abrams Books for Young Readers • New York

Here we see a typical resident of Blinsh. His name is Herman Renfrew, and he is a vampire. Herman is returning home from a trip, and he is greeted by his pets.

Herman works as a clerk in the Blinsh city hall. His pets are dogs, or possibly small wolves, and a couple of mice, little children of the night; they love their master.

Herman has not had time to shop for supper, so he goes to the nearby all-night doughnut shop. In the parking lot, on an impulse, he bites a citizen named Jonas Papooshnik.

We join a scene of Blinsh on a rainy morning. Can you see Mr. Papooshnik still asleep in his house?

Here we see Mr. Papooshnik about to try out his new night-vision glasses. The rain has stopped, and there are quite a few wolves and other animals wandering about.

Possibly Mr. Papooshnik will be able to see them.

Wearing the night-vision glasses,
Mr. Papooshnik spies on his neighbor,
Cowboy Bob. Mr. Papooshnik thinks
Cowboy Bob will not know he is there.
Of course, the porch light is on,
and Cowboy Bob can see him
perfectly well.

Mr. Papooshnik departs.
At the same time, a woman named
Grimna Farforshnik, mother of six, samples
a spinach, sardine, and peach doughnut.
She is disappointed.

We visit the police station in Blinsh. Herman is there. He has brought the officers some green olive and applesauce doughnuts. The police are popular with the citizens, who often drop by to see them. The police feel it is their duty to eat the doughnuts.

POLICE

BLINSH POLICE

Outside the police station, we see Cowboy Bob in the classic pose of a vampire. But he is not a vampire.

BLINSH POLICE

PNK·109

A genuine vampire can be seen on the roof of the police station. Can you tell why he is the real thing, and Cowboy Bob is not?

Mr. Papooshnik appears to be floating in the air.
Numerous normal-type Pinksylvanians have learned to do
this for short periods, perhaps from vampire neighbors?

The community room in city hall on a typical evening.

Parents are helping their children with homework, some citizens are chatting, others are eating doughnuts, discussing issues of the day, being bitten by vampires (or in the case of vampires, biting).

It is a scene many readers will find familiar.

There is much to do at night in Blinsh,

and Blinshites, particularly the vampire ones, love the night.

In fine weather, citizens stroll, float, fly, visit with their neighbors,

or possibly attend the drive-in open-air movie theater.

Almost everyone in town attends the annual Midnight Madness sale at Onion King, a discount market on the outskirts of Blinsh.

The produce is stale, but the prices are sensational.

This is the office where
Mr. Renfrew works.
Mr. Renfrew does not
appear to be present.

Here is the same office at night, when normally no one is present. We do not know the identity of the lady visiting.

Halloween! This holiday is celebrated in Blinsh—and all of Pinksylvania—like nowhere else in the world.

In fact, the people of Blinsh cannot limit their celebrating to a single date on the calendar.

Worried families look for loved ones who never came home,

and the streets are crowded with vampires
and regular citizens staying up all night.

Some aspects of civic life in Blinsh. We see the all-vampire fire department at work,

the local football team, the dramatic society,

BLINSH BEAR CLAWS

GO CLAWS!

a game of vampire basketball, and an example of the work of the Society for the Prevention of Cruelty to Raccoons.

In general, the inhabitants of Blinsh are happy and content, with the possible exception of Otto Van Helsing, an amateur garlic fancier with perhaps a somewhat sour disposition. Yet his neighbors like him, and some may bite him.

Now, we depart from Blinsh, and pay a visit to the nearby city of Blorsh.

Blorsh is easy to reach by train, bus, automobile, or horse cart,

and some energetic vampires fly there under their own power. Blorsh has fine dining, flavors of doughnuts unknown in Blinsh, and concerts by popular vampire groups.

Blorsh is a more free-spirited place than Blinsh. The residents have a more relaxed style of living and make full use of Blorsh's beautiful city park.

The fun never stops in Blorsh,

the city that never sleeps . . . at night.

There are not enough pages in this book to do justice to the capital of Pinksylvani, the magnificent city of Farshningle.

Let it suffice to say that Farshningle has everything British and Blorsh
have, including charming residents of the vampire and non-vampire sort,
a vast variety of disgusting doughnuts, and the Pinksylvanian Parliament,
housed in a beautiful building decorated with many electric light bulbs.

But there is no place like home, which is to say there is no place like Blinsh. It is here we find the true culture of Pinksylvania and the true friendship and tolerance between normal folk and the undead. Now, we must bid a reluctant farewell to Blinsh and say to all our Pinksylvanian friends, "Hey, take your teeth off my neck!"